For Kathy Henderson,
who had the idea

The publishers are grateful for permission to reproduce the following material:

From **First Things First** by Charlotte Voake.
Copyright © 1988 by Charlotte Voake.
By permission of Little, Brown and Company.

From **Things I Like** by Anthony Browne.
Copyright © 1988 by Anthony Browne.
Reprinted by permission of Alfred A. Knopf, Inc.

Illustrations from **Michael Foreman's Mother Goose,**
copyright © 1991 by Michael Foreman, reprinted
by permission of Harcourt Brace & Company.

From **Monkey See, Monkey Do** by Helen Oxenbury.
Copyright © 1982 by Helen Oxenbury.
Used by permission of Dial Books for Young Readers,
a division of Penguin Books USA Inc.

Reprinted with the permission of Little Simon, an imprint
of Simon & Schuster Children's Publishing Division
from **Pippo Gets Lost** by Helen Oxenbury. Text and
illustrations copyright © 1989 Helen Oxenbury.

Illustrations from **Pet Animals** and **Farm Animals**
by Lucy Cousins. Copyright © 1990 by Lucy Cousins.
By permission of Tambourine Books, a division of
William Morrow & Co., Inc..

Text copyright © year of publication
of individual authors
Illustrations copyright © year of publication
of individual illustrators

All rights reserved.

First U.S. edition 1995

Library of Congress Catalog Card Number TK

ISBN 1-56402-655-8

10 9 8 7 6 5 4 3 2 1

Printed in Mexico

Candlewick Press
2067 Massachusetts Avenue
Cambridge, MA 02140

CANDLEWICK PRESS
CAMBRIDGE, MASSACHUSETTS

BABY BEAR'S TREASURY

25 STORIES FOR THE VERY, VERY YOUNG

The Green Queen

The green queen lay in he

But she had to go out, so she got up

her black jacket,  and her yellow

and orange and indigo scarf. And...

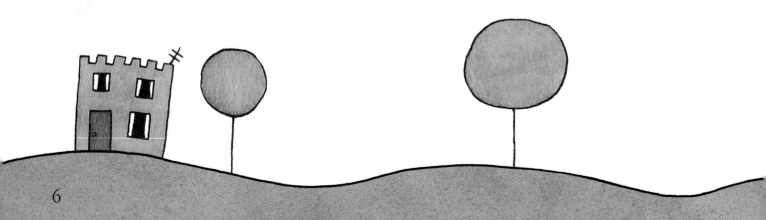

6

Nick Sharratt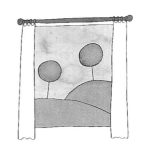

red bed and looked at the gray day.

 She put on her blue shoes,

and pink and turquoise and brown

out she went.

When We Went to the Park

Shirley Hughes

When Grandpa and I put on our coats and went to the park . . .

1  We saw one black cat sitting on a wall,

2  Two big girls licking ice-cream cones,

3  Three ladies chatting on a bench,

4  Four babies in strollers,

5 Five children playing in the sandbox,

6  Six runners running,

7

Seven dogs chasing one another,

8

Eight boys kicking a ball,

9

Nine ducks swimming in the pond,

10

Ten birds swooping in the sky, and so many leaves
that I couldn't count them all.

On the way back we saw
the black cat again.
Then we went home for dinner.

10

Helen Oxenbury

Sometimes Pippo gets lost
and I have to look for him.
I asked Mommy if she'd
seen Pippo, and she
said I should look in
my toy-chest again.
Pippo wasn't there,
but I found his
scarf.

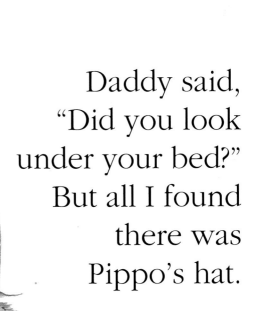

Daddy said,
"Did you look
under your bed?"
But all I found
there was
Pippo's hat.

11

I got really worried about Pippo and thought I might never see him again.

Mommy said that Pippo couldn't be far away and said that we should look in the living room.

And that's where he was all the time, in the bookcase.

I told Pippo to tell me before he goes away next time.

13

Let's

Can you find your ears?

Can you bite your toes?

Can you find your eyes?

Amy MacDonald

14

Do It

Can you play peek-a-boo?

Can you touch your nose?

Can you wave bye-bye?

illustrated by Maureen Roffey

Where's My Mommy?

Colin and Jacqui Hawkins

MOTHER GOOSE

LITTLE BOY BLUE

Little Boy Blue,
   Come blow your horn,
The sheep's in the meadow,
   The cow's in the corn;
But where is the boy
   Who looks after the sheep?
He's under a haystack,
   Fast asleep.
Will you wake him?
   No, not I,
For if I do,
   He's sure to cry.

Three poems illustrated by
Michael Foreman

TO THE MAGPIE

Magpie, magpie, flutter and flee,
Turn up your tail and good luck come to me.

BAA, BAA, BLACK SHEEP

Baa, baa, black sheep,
   Have you any wool?
Yes sir, yes sir,
   Three bags full:
One for the master,
   And one for the dame,
And one for the little boy
   Who lives down the lane.

Here Come the Babies

What does a baby do?

jumble

juggle

jump

bang

burp

bump

totter

tumble

throw

gurgle

giggle

grow

Catherine and Laurence Anholt

What are babies like?

Babies kick
and babies crawl,

Slide their potties down the hall.

Babies smile
and babies yell,

This one has
a funny smell.

animals Lucy Cousins

donkey

duck

hen

pig

rabbit

cat

goose

rooster

You're Adorable

A you're a-dor-a-ble B you're so beau-ti-ful C you're a cu-tie full of   charms

D you're a dar-ling and E you're ex-cit-ing and F you're a feath-er in   my   arms

G you look good to me H you're so hea-ven-ly I you're the one I   i-dol-ize

J we're like Jack and Jill K you're so kiss-a-ble L is the love-light in   your   eyes

24   *A song by Buddy Kaye, Fred Wise, and Sidney Lippman*

M N O P I could go on— all day Q R

S T al-pha-bet-i-cally speak-ing you're o-kay— U made my life com-plete

V means you're ver-y sweet W——— X Y Z— It's

fun to wan-der through the al-pha-bet with you to tell you what you mean to me!—

illustrated by Martha Alexander

25

OLD MOTHER HUBBARD

**Old Mother Hubbard
Went to the cupboard**

To fetch her poor dog a bone;
But when she got there,
The cupboard was bare,
And so the poor dog had none.

She went to the baker's
To buy him some bread;
But when she came back,
The poor dog was dead.

She went to the fishmonger's
To buy him some fish;
But when she came back,
He was licking the dish.

She went to the undertaker's
To buy him a coffin;
But when she came back,
The poor dog was laughing.

She took a clean dish
To get him some tripe;
But when she came back,
He was smoking a pipe.

She went to the hatter's
To buy him a hat;
But when she came back,
He was feeding the cat.

illustrated by Elizabeth Wood

She went to the tailor's
To buy him a coat;
But when she came back,
He was riding a goat.

She went to the cobbler's
To buy him some shoes;
But when she came back,
He was reading the news.

She went to the seamstress
To buy him some linen;
But when she came back,
The dog was a-spinning.

She went to the barber's
To buy him a wig;
But when she came back,
He was dancing a jig.

She went to the hosier's
To buy him some hose;
But when she came back,
He was dressed in his clothes.

The dame made a curtsy,
The dog made a bow;
The dame said, "Your servant,"
The dog said, "Bow-wow."

I Love Animals

Flora McDonnell

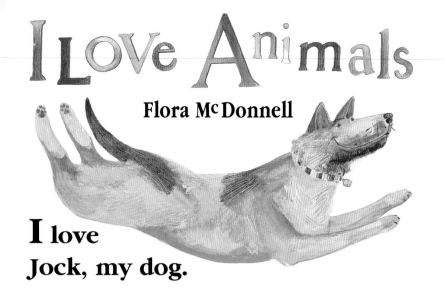

I love
Jock, my dog.

I love the ducks
waddling to the water.

I love
the donkey
braying
"hee-haw!"

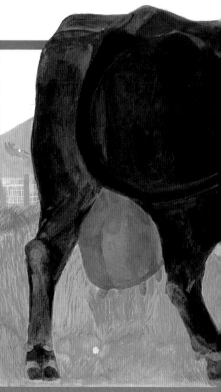

I love
the pony
rolling
over and
over.

I love the turkey
strutting around
the yard.

I love the pig with all her little piglets.

I love the hens hopping up and down.

I love the cow swishing her tail.

I love the goat racing across the field.

I love the sheep bleating to her lamb.

I love all the animals.

I hope they love me.

Sleeping

peeping

tickling

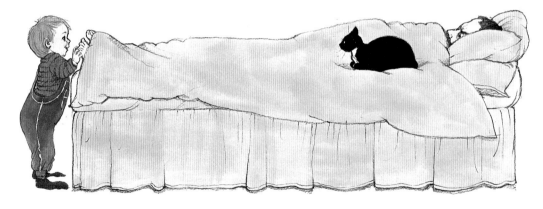

climbing up

Jan Ormerod

bouncing

pulling his nose

cuddling

31

HUMPTY DUMPTY

illustrated by Julie Lacome

Humpty Dumpty
Sat on a wall,
Humpty Dumpty
Had a great fall.

All the king's horses
And all the king's men
Couldn't put Humpty
Together again.

My Cat Jack

Patricia Casey

My cat Jack is a yawning cat.
He's a stretching-down cat. He's a stretching-up cat.

My cat Jack is a scratching cat.
He's a curling cat. He's a lapping cat.

My cat Jack is a purring cat,
a rough-tongued cat, a washing cat.

He's a cat who likes washing all over.

My cat Jack is a playing cat.
He's a pouncing cat. He's an acrobat cat.

And sometimes he's a silly old cat.
I love him, my cat Jack.

Clara Vulliamy **Blue Hat**

orange gloves

blue hat

red coat

brown sweater

Red Coat

black shoes

 green socks

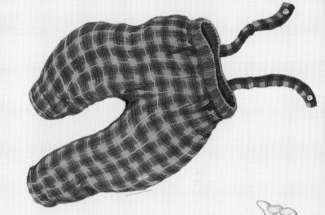

purple overalls

 pink T-shirt

yellow undershirt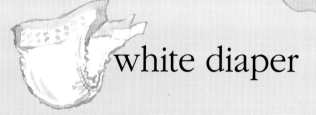

white diaper

. . . all gone!

37

Animals

Helen Oxenbury

39

Jill the Farmer
and Her Friends

Nick Butterworth

Pete is a mechanic.

What does he use?

Betty is a baker.

What does she sell?

Fred is a garbageman.

What does he collect?

Anna is a doctor.

Why has she come?

Jim is a messenger.

What does he ride?

Gray plane

CHARLOTTE VOAKE'S

COLORS

PURPLE

RED

Brown
trailer

Red
truck

42

Green tractor

Blue train

Black

ORANGE

GREEN

BLUE YELLOW PINK BROWN

Yellow boat

Pink car

Black-bike

FOUR BLACK

Four black puppies in a basket, fast asleep.

One black puppy
waking up.

One black puppy
going for a walk.

PUPPIES

by
Sally Grindley

illustrated by
Clive Scruton

One black puppy
pulling on an apron.

One shopping basket
falling down.

CRASH!

45

Three black puppies running in to take a look.

Three black puppies
see . . . A GHOST.

One white puppy chasing
three black puppies.

All four puppies running round and round.

All four puppies running back to bed.

All four puppies in a basket, fast asleep.

cluck baa

hiss

cluck

hoot

croak

neigh

48

Noah's Ark

A long time ago there lived a man called Noah.

Noah was a good man, who trusted in God.

There were also many wicked people in the world.

God wanted to punish the wicked people,

so he said to Noah,

"I shall make a flood of water and wash all the wicked people away. Build an ark for your family and all the animals."

Noah worked for years and years and years to build the ark.

At last the ark was finished.

Noah and his family gathered lots of food.

Then the animals came,

two by two,

two by two,

into the ark.

retold and illustrated by Lucy Cousins

When the ark was full, Noah felt a drop of rain. It rained and rained and rained. It rained for forty days and forty nights. The world was covered with water. At last the rain stopped and the sun came out. Noah sent a dove to find dry land. The dove came back with a leafy twig. "Hurrah!" shouted Noah. "The flood has ended." But many more days passed before the ark came to rest on dry land. Then Noah and all the animals came safely out of the ark . . . and life began again on the earth.

51

Bumpety Bump

A Lap Game Poem

Kathy Henderson   *illustrated by Carol Thompson*

The baby went for a ride,
***a-bumpety-
bumpety-bump!***

She rode in her sister's arms,
***a-slumpety-
slumpety-slump!***

She rode on her
grandpa's knee,
***a-tumpety-
tumpety-tump!***

She rode on her mother's hip,
***a-lumpety-
lumpety-lump!***

She rode on her uncle's neck,
***a-humpety-
humpety-hump!***

And flew high up in the air,
***a-jumpety-
jumpety-jump!***

She rode around and
about and then . . .
went back to sleep
in her crib again.

Things
I Like

Anthony Browne

*This is me
and this is
what I like:*

Painting . . .
and riding my bike.

Playing with toys,
and dressing up.

Climbing trees . . .
and kicking a ball.

Hiding . . .
and acrobatics.

Making a cake . . .
and watching TV.

Going to birthday
parties, and being
with my friends.

Having a bath . . .
hearing a
bedtime story . . .

and dreaming.

Where's Willy?

 Go hide, Willy.
Here I come!

 What a funny bag!
It has feet.

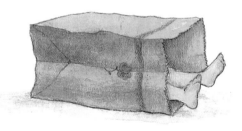

 That bag
walks.

It's following me.
It's running!

The bag's fallen down.

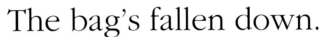

It's Willy!
I found you!

57

GO TO

It was time for Bartholomew to go to bed.

"Ba, time for bed," George said.

"Nah!" said Bartholomew.

Nah

George said, "Brush your teeth and go to bed." "Nah!" said Bartholomew.

58

BED!

Virginia Miller

"Have you brushed your teeth yet, Ba?"
"Nah!" said Bartholomew, beginning to cry.

"Come on, Ba, into bed!"
George said.
"Nah!" said Bartholomew.
"Nah, nah, nah, nah,
NAH!" said Bartholomew.

to bed!"

orge said in a big voice.
Bartholomew got into bed.

He giggled and wriggled, he hid and tiggled,

he cuddled and huggled, he snuggled and sighed.